For Spyro and Stelio and best friends everywhere

WE ARE BEST FRIENDS

by Aliki

A MULBERRY PAPERBACK BOOK
New York

5 6 7 8 9 10

Library of Congress Cataloging in Publication Data
Aliki.   We are best friends.
Summary: When Robert's best friend Peter
moves away, both are unhappy, but they
learn that they can make new friends and
still remain best friends.
[1. Friendship—Fiction]   I. Title.
PZ7.A397We   [E]   81-6549
ISBN 0-688-07037-X   AACR2

Peter came to tell Robert the news.

"I am moving away," he said.

"You can't move away," said Robert.

"We are best friends."

"I am moving far away," said Peter.

"What will you do without me?" asked Robert.

"Who will you play with?"

"We will live in a new house," said Peter.

"You will miss my birthday party!" said Robert.

"I will be going to a new school," said Peter.
"Who will you fight with?" asked Robert.
"Nobody fights like best friends."
"I will make new friends," said Peter.
"You can't move away," said Robert.
"You will miss me too much."

But Peter moved away.

There was nothing to do without Peter.

There was no one to play with.

There was no one to share with.

There was no one to fight with.
Not the way best friends fight.
There was no fun anymore.
"I'll bet Peter doesn't even remember me,"
said Robert.
"It's a good thing he's not here.
I'd have to punch him one."

"Hello. My name is Will," said a new face.

I don't like freckles, thought Robert.

"I used to go to another school," said Will.

I don't like glasses, thought Robert.

"My friends are all there," said Will.

I don't like silly names like Will,
thought Robert.

"It was fun," said Will.

"Not boring like this place."

A letter came for Robert.
A letter from Peter.

DEAR ROBERT,
I HOPE YOU STILL REMEMBER ME.
I LIKE MY NEW HOUSE NOW.
I LIKE MY NEW SCHOOL NOW.
AT FIRST I DIDN'T LIKE ANYTHING.
BUT NOW I HAVE A FRIEND, ALEX.
YOU ARE MY BEST FRIEND,
BUT ALEX IS NICE.

IT IS FUN TO HAVE SOMEONE
TO PLAY WITH AGAIN.
IT'S NOT SO LONELY.
                LOVE, PETER

Robert drew Peter a letter.
He drew two friends building a fort.
He drew them playing with their cars.
He drew them riding their bikes.
He wrote:

IF YOU WERE HERE,
THIS IS WHAT WE'D BE DOING.
BUT YOU'RE NOT.

Then he wrote:

THERE IS A NEW BOY IN SCHOOL.
HE HAS FRECKLES.

Robert saw Will by the fence.

"Did you lose something?" he asked.

"I thought I saw a frog," said Will.

"That's funny, looking for a frog," said Robert.

"What's funny about it?

I like frogs," said Will.

"I used to have a pet frog named Greenie.

He'd wait for me by the pond near where I lived.

He must miss me a lot."

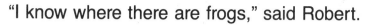

"I know where there are frogs," said Robert.

"Right in my garden."

"You're just saying that," said Will.

"I mean it," said Robert.

"You can see for yourself."

"If I had a frog in my garden, I'd share it," said Will.

"That's what I'm doing," said Robert.

Robert and Will rode home together.

They went straight into the garden.

The frogs were there.

One leaped under a bush, and Will caught it.

"I'll call you Greenie the Second," he said.

"You like me already, don't you?"

"The frogs lay their eggs here every year,"
 said Robert.
"It's almost time.
 My friend Peter used to come
 watch the tadpoles.
 He called them Inkywiggles.
 He'll miss them."
"Why?" asked Will.
"He moved away," said Robert.
"Just about the time you came.
 I write him letters."
"Then you can write about the Inkywiggles,"
 said Will.
 They laughed.
"I haven't had so much fun since I moved here,"
 said Will.
"Neither have I," said Robert.

Robert wrote to Peter.

DEAR PETER,
I CAN'T WAIT UNTIL SUMMER
WHEN YOU COME TO VISIT.
THE NEW BOY IS CALLED WILL.
I SHOWED HIM THE FROGS.
HE HAD A PET ONE NEAR HIS HOME.
BUT HE HAD TO MOVE AWAY, LIKE YOU.
HE THINKS INKYWIGGLES IS FUNNY.
I'LL WRITE WHEN THEY HATCH.

LOVE, ROBERT.

P.S. HOW IS ALEX?
P.P.S. SEE YOU SOON.

Robert mailed the letter,
then rode over to Will's house to play.